To Ben, my pants-tastic illustrator ~ C. F.

For Ruth, with all my love ~ B. C.

ALADDIN

An imprint of Simon & Schuster Children's Publishing Division

1230 Avenue of the Americas, New York, NY 10020

First Aladdin hardcover edition September 2013

Text copyright © 2013 by Claire Freedman

Illustrations copyright © 2013 by Ben Cort

Originally published in Great Britain in 2013 by Simon & Schuster UK Ltd.

For information about special discounts for bulk purchases, please contact Simon & Schuster Special Sales

at 1-866-506-1949 or business@simonandschuster.com.

The Simon & Schuster Speakers Bureau can bring authors to your live event. For more information or to book an event contact the

Simon & Schuster Speakers Bureau at 1-866-248-3049 or visit our website at www.simonspeakers.com.

Manufactured in Slovenia 0616 SUK

6 8 10 9 7 5

This book has been cataloged with the Library of Congress

ISBN 978-1-4424-8512-9

ISBN 978-1-4424-8513-6 (eBook)

Pirates Love Underpants

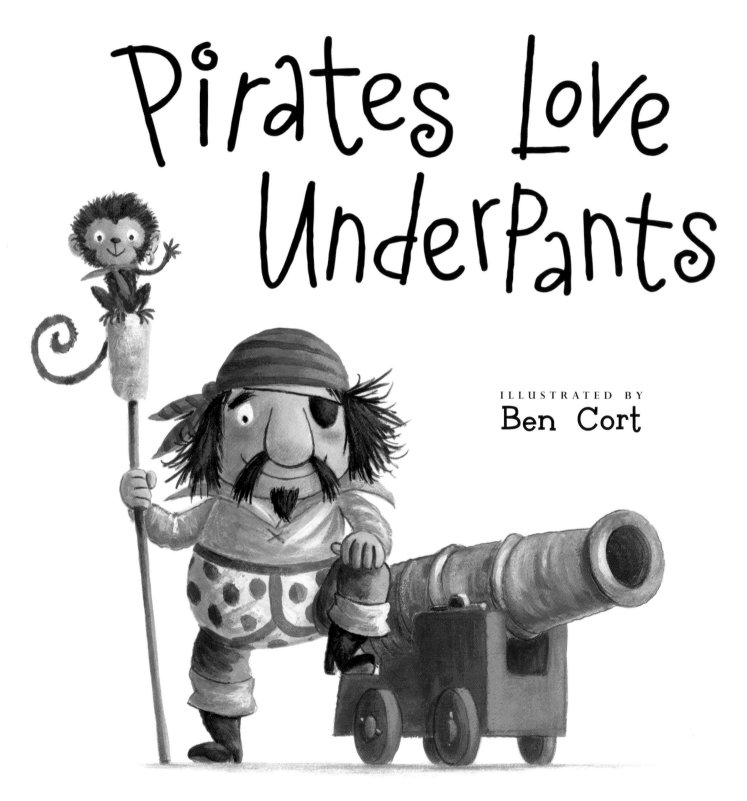

ILLUSTRATED BY
Ben Cort

CLAIRE FREEDMAN

aladdin

NEW YORK   LONDON   TORONTO   SYDNEY   NEW DELHI

These pirates SO love underpants,
they're on a special quest
To find the fabled Pants Of Gold,
for the captain's treasure chest.

"Anchors aweigh!" the captain cries.
"Hoist up *Black Bloomer*'s sail!
Unfurl the secret treasure map.
Pants pirates NEVER fail!"

Black Bloomer bobs upon the waves.

The captain shouts, "Hooray!

Sharks in fancy underpants!

We've found Big Knickers Bay!"

The pirates grab their shiny swords,
and row their boats to shore.
"Yikes, me hearties, what is this?
Someone's been 'ere before!"

The footprints lead through shifting dunes,
across the Three Pants Ridge.
"Snap! Snap!" snarl the hungry crocs
beneath the Long-John Bridge!

The pirates wade through
gurgling swamps . . .
through caves as black
as night.
They trek through
prickly undergrowth,
then, GULP!
Oh, what a sight!

"We're here too late!" the pirates gasp.
"ANOTHER pirate crew!
They've found the golden underpants.
What are we going to do?"

The captain has a cunning plan.

It's clever! It's fantastic!

"Grab their fancy underpants and . . .

CUT through the elastic!"

As the rival pirates sleep,
 they SNIP round on tiptoe.
But help! The captain's parrot SQUAWKS,
 and wakes them up—Oh no!

"Grab those pants!" the captain roars.
"They're after us—oooh-arrr!"
But with their pants around their feet,
they don't get very far!

"Yo-ho! Ho-ho!" The pirates dance.
"Fine treasure fills our hold.
But what's the booty we love best?
The glittering PANTS OF GOLD!"

So when you put your pants on, check
    the elastic is in place.
Or like those silly pirates found—
    you'll have a bright red face!